THE ESCAPE OF MARVIN THE APE

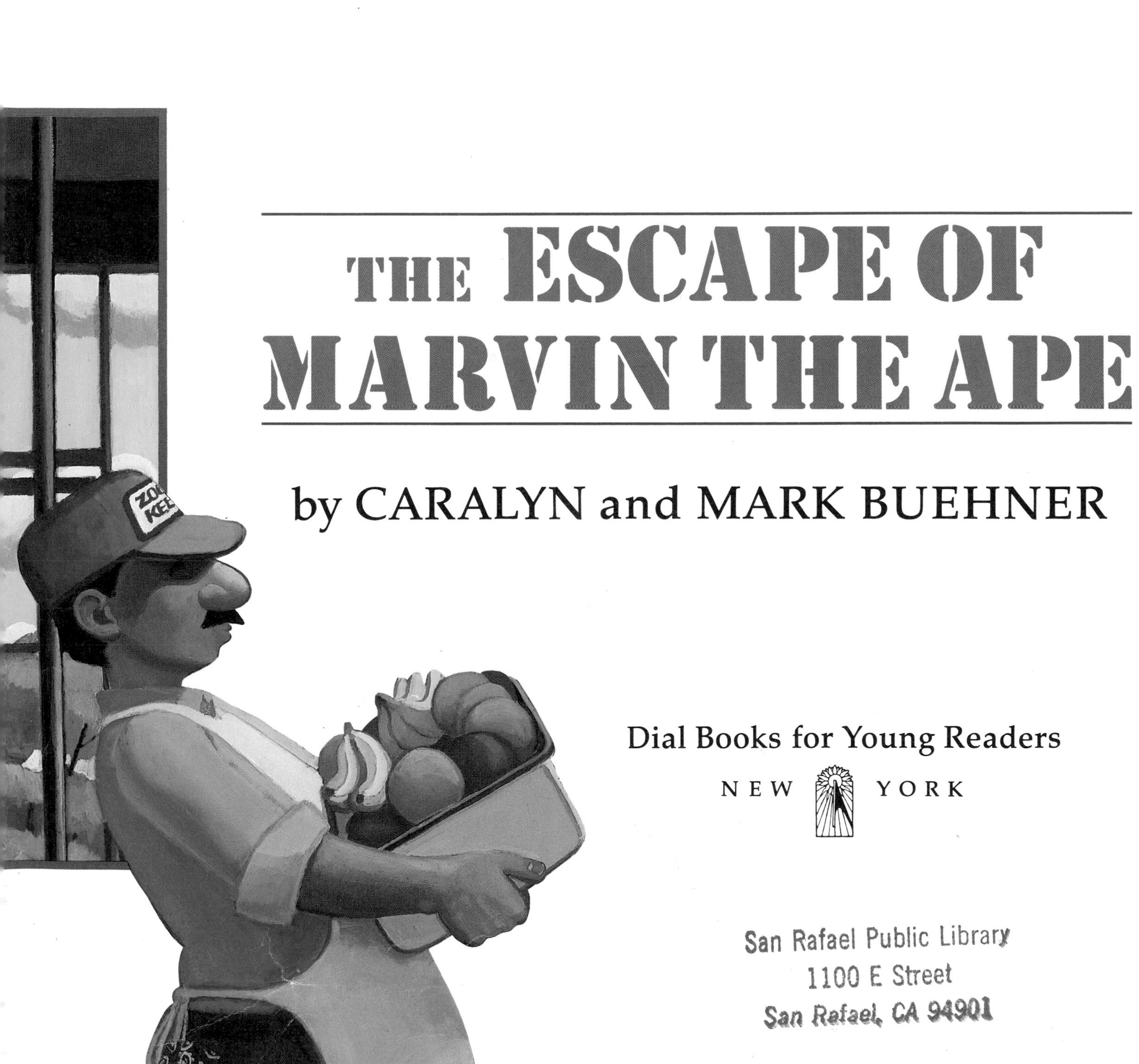

THE ESCAPE OF MARVIN THE APE

by CARALYN and MARK BUEHNER

Dial Books for Young Readers
NEW YORK

It was feeding time, and when the zookeeper wasn't looking, Marvin...

POPC

slipped out.
The zookeeper couldn't find Marvin anywhere.

Neither could the police.

Foot Pains?
TO NEW YORK
VIEW POINTS
CITY
BROOKLYN
MONEY IN BUSINESS

Feeling rather hungry, Marvin stopped for a bite.
"Ah, the Jungle Fruit Platter," said the waiter.
"An excellent choice!"

There was a wonderful park nearby. Marvin loved to swing.

MUSEUM MAP

At the museum Marvin was delighted to find a painting done by his Uncle Hairy.

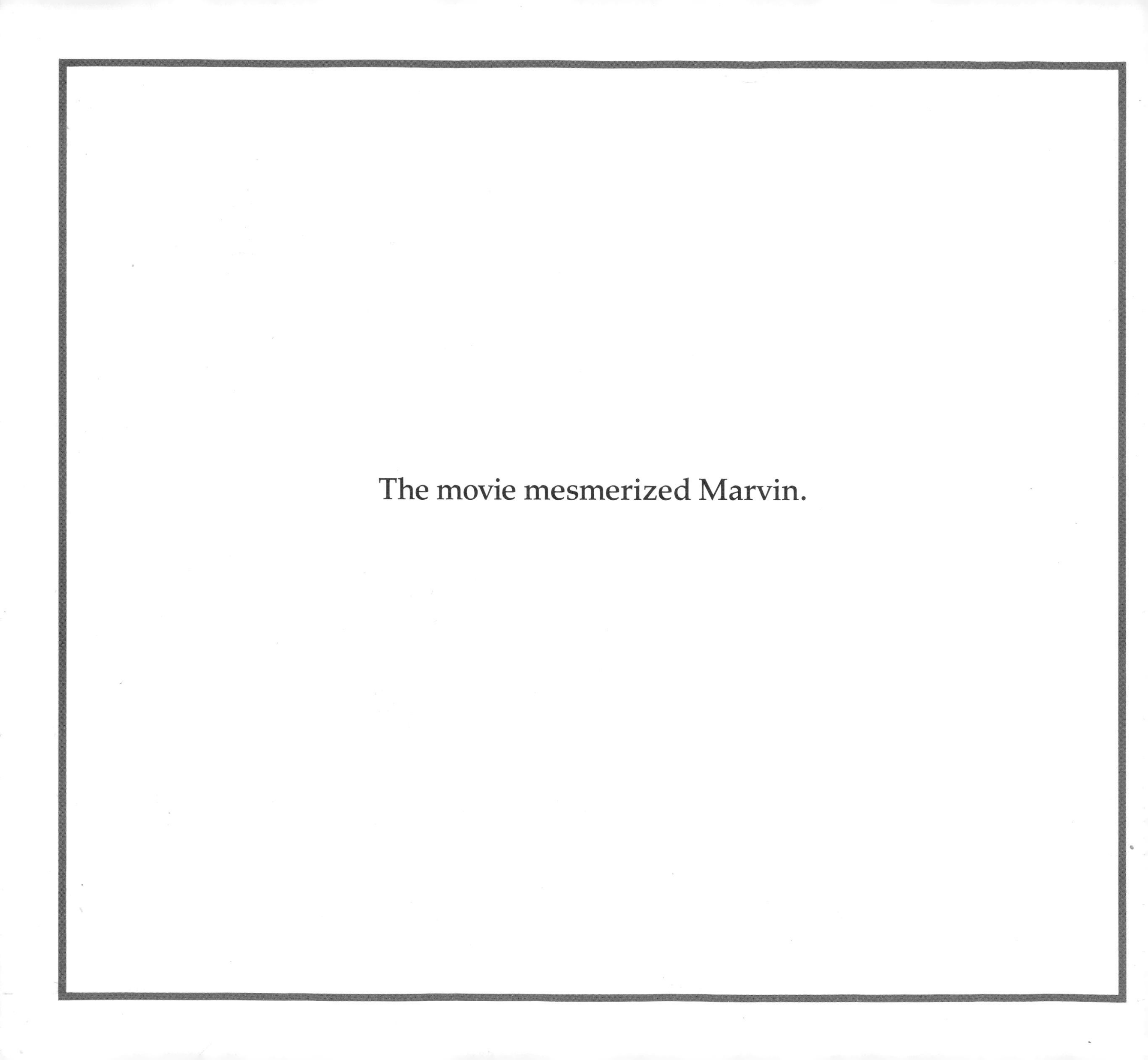

The movie mesmerized Marvin.

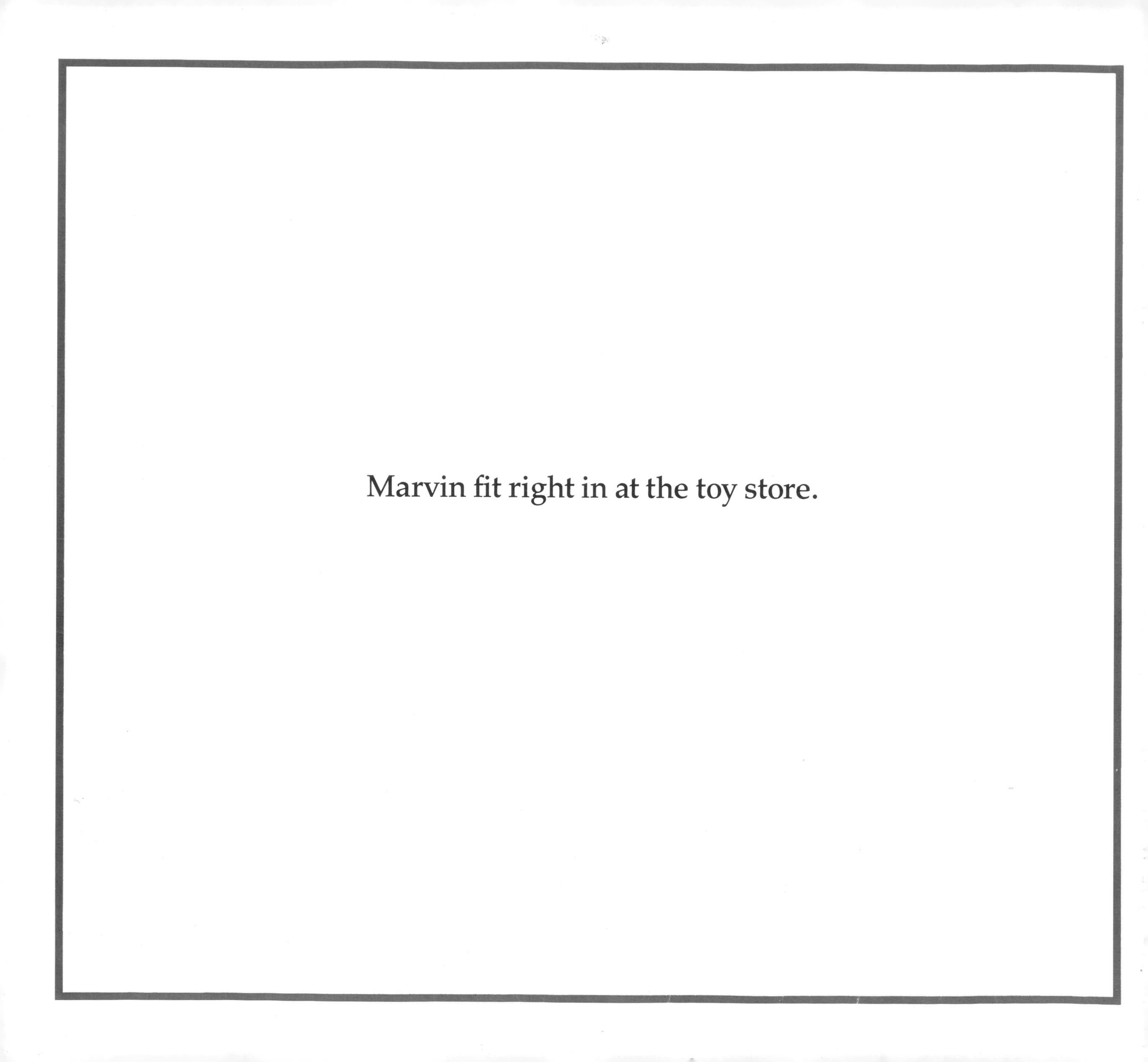

Marvin fit right in at the toy store.

EXIT

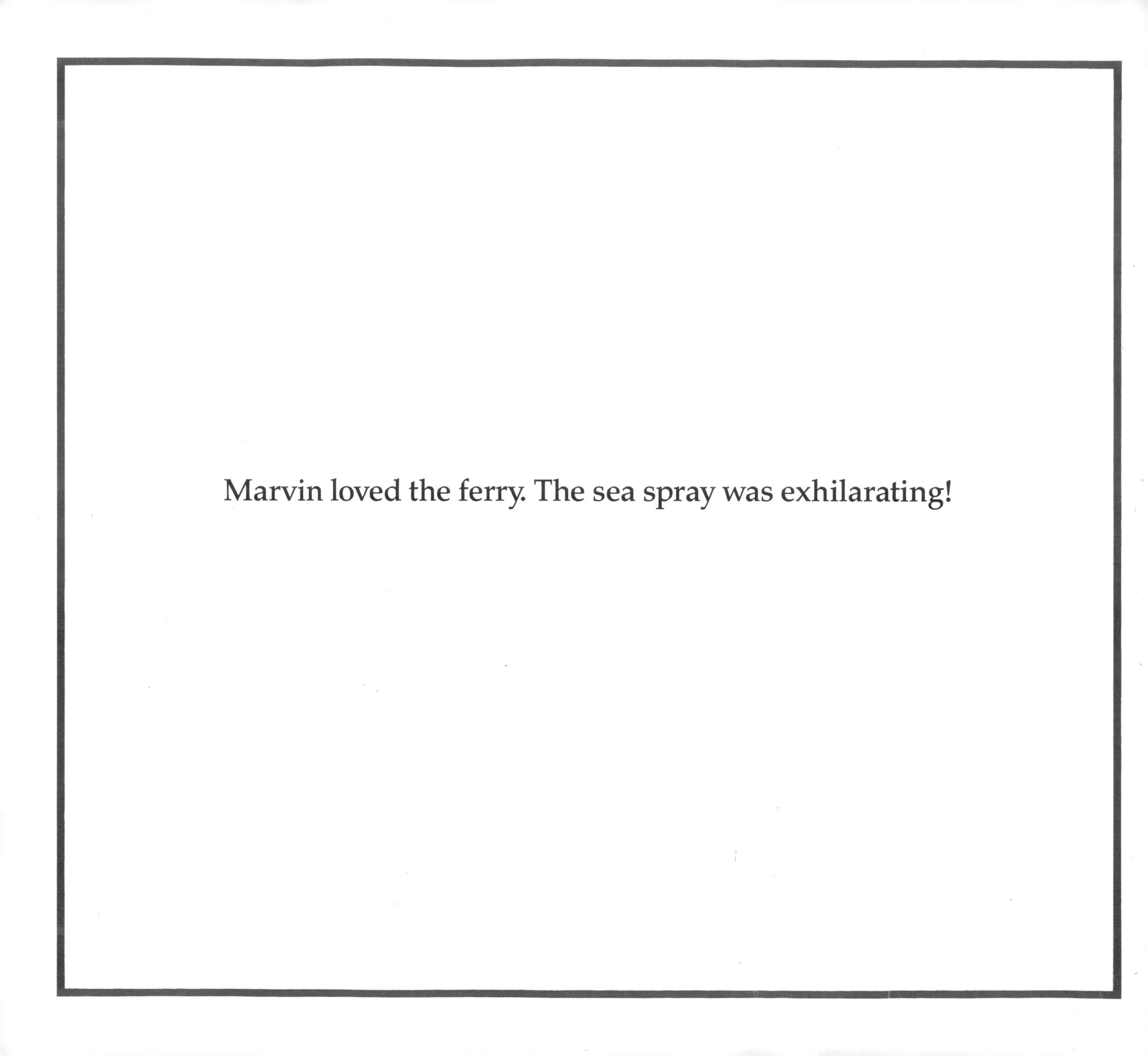

Marvin loved the ferry. The sea spray was exhilarating!

erry

PIZZA
FRUIT MARKET

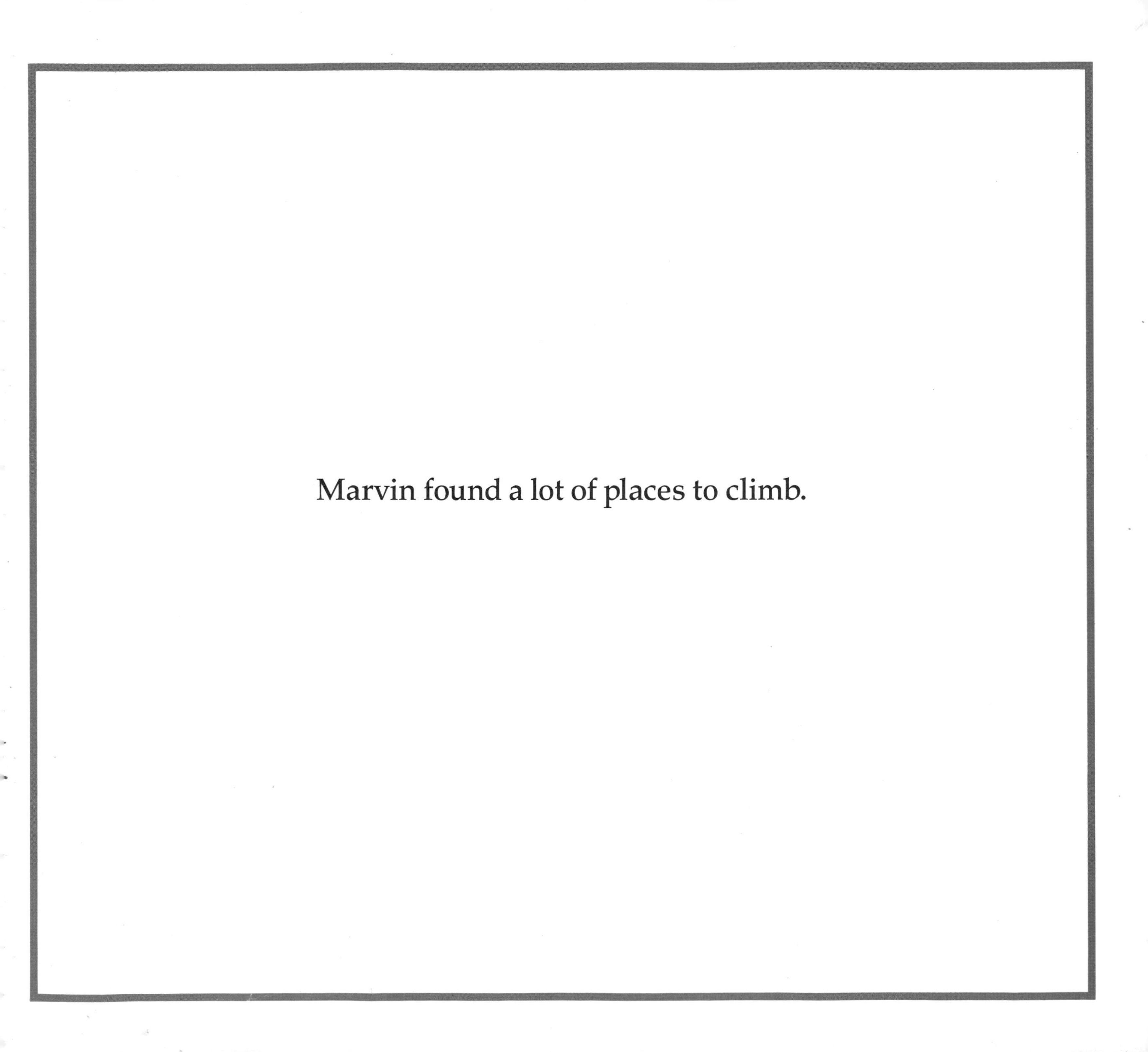

Marvin found a lot of places to climb.

HOTDOGS

At a ball game Marvin
caught a pop-up foul.

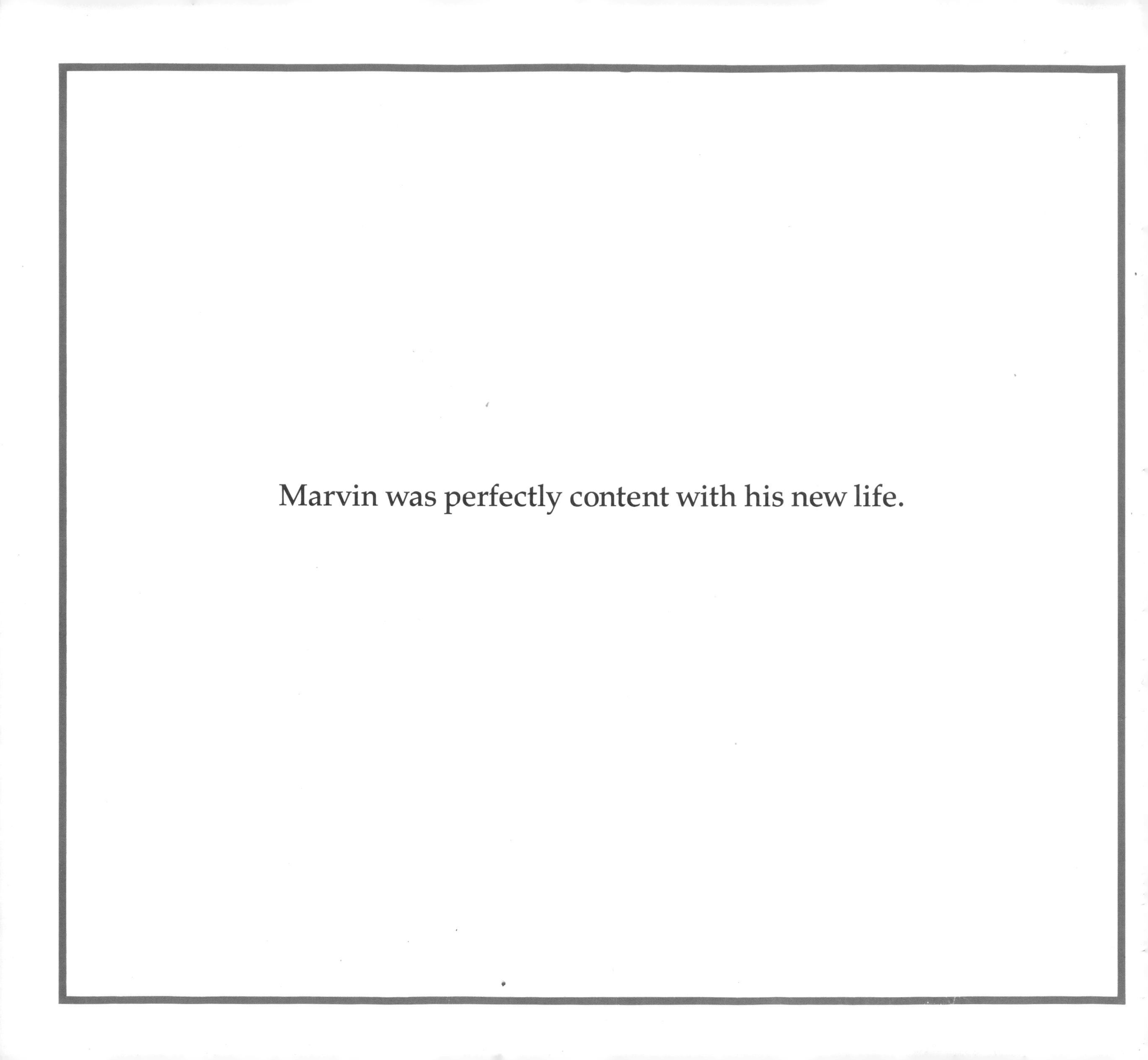

Marvin was perfectly content with his new life.

I ♥
NEW

Meanwhile, back at the zoo, it was feeding time and while the zookeeper's head was turned, Helvetica . . .

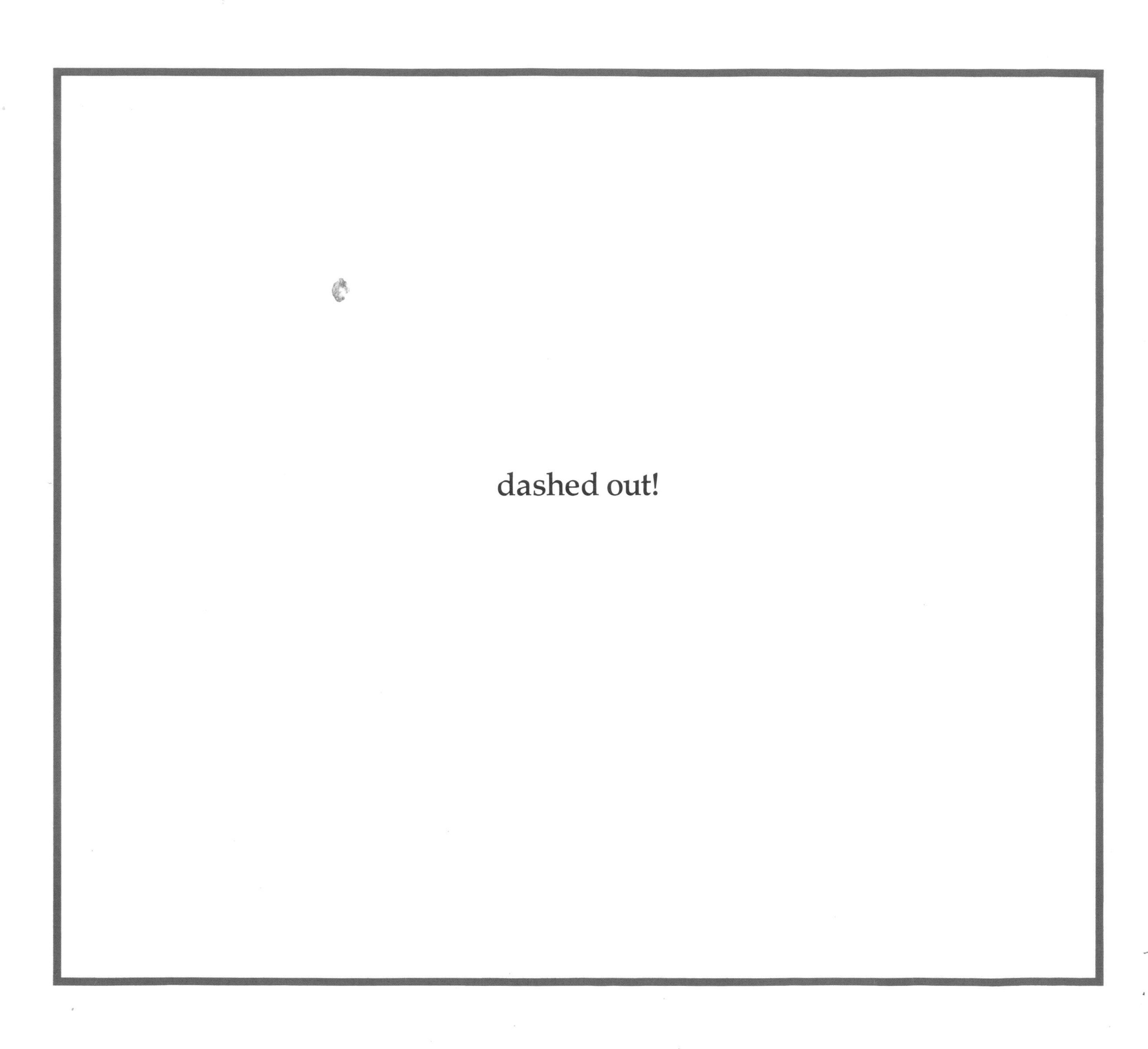

dashed out!

HIPPO
GORILLA
EXIT
TIGER

To Heidi, Grant, and Sarah

C. B. and M. B.

Published by Dial Books for Young Readers
A Division of Penguin Books USA Inc.
375 Hudson Street • New York, New York 10014

Designed by Mara Nussbaum
Printed in the U.S.A.
First Edition
1 3 5 7 9 10 8 6 4 2

Library of Congress Cataloging in Publication Data
Buehner, Caralyn.
The escape of Marvin the ape / by Caralyn and Mark Buehner;
pictures by Mark Buehner.—1st ed.
p. cm.
Summary: Marvin the ape slips out of the zoo and finds he likes it
on the outside, where he easily blends into city lifestyles.
ISBN 0-8037-1123-9.—ISBN 0-8037-1124-7 (lib. bdg.)
[1. Apes—Fiction. 2. City and town life—Fiction.]
I. Buehner, Mark. II. Title.
PZ7.B884Es 1992 [E]—dc20 91-10795 CIP AC

The art for this book was prepared by using oil paints over acrylics.
It was then color-separated and reproduced in red, yellow, blue, and black halftones.